From Red River to Blue Danube

Kieu Bich Hau

(Revised by Paul Christiansen)

Ukiyoto Publishing

All global publishing rights are held by

Ukiyoto Publishing

Published in 2023

Content Copyright © Kieu Bich Hau
ISBN 9789360167363

*All rights reserved.
No part of this publication may be reproduced,
transmitted, or stored in a retrieval system, in any
form by any means, electronic, mechanical,
photocopying, recording or otherwise, without the
prior permission of the publisher.*

The moral rights of the author have been asserted.

*This is a work of fiction. Names, characters, businesses,
places, events, locales, and incidents are either the
products of the author's imagination or used in a
fictitious manner. Any resemblance to actual persons,
living or dead, or actual events is purely coincidental.*

*This book is sold subject to the condition that it shall
not by way of trade or otherwise, be lent, resold, hired
out or otherwise circulated, without the publisher's
prior consent, in any form of binding or cover other
than that in which it is published.*

For HJB with my great love and gratitude.

Contents

The only road I know	1
Cry	2
Ash everywhere	3
Love seeds	4
Drunk afternoon	5
The source	6
Danger	7
Changes	8
Peace	9
The new truth	10
Be alert	11
Two moons	12
Lost in the river of time	14
Soulmateship	15
Pathless	16
Release myself	17
Alive word	18
The beauty of Petofi	19
The divine emptiness	20
Walk into our fate	23
Flying on golden wings	24
Transcendent union	25
After a pipe	27

Collapse of humanity	28
The death	29
Enough!	31
Cut myself	32
Man and Woman	33
Two books	34
Grape and Rose	35
Step into the Unknown	36
Summer night at Bartok Bela* street	37
O man	39
Secret box	40
Danube late afternoon	42
The song of Red River	44
Ao dai* at Buda castle	45
Love & Gratitude	46
Boiling sea	48
Daily chant	49
Fix yourself	51
Illusion	52
Hotel President	53
Wisdom	55
Be calm	56
Secret Song of Solitude Soul	57
The ash in me	59
M.U.M*	60
Never be picky	61

Bat Trang, holding hands	62
You are a strong wind	63
Spirit	64
Purification	65
HJB	66
Doless	67
Senseless	68
Robots never gets angry	69
Touch you in the distance	70
Living metaphors	72
Pray	74
Call girl	75
A storm of love	78
Can Gio* – the little paradise	79
About the Author	*82*

The only road I know

My darling, don't leave me
without you, I will lose my way

I won't know where to go
I don't know which road in this city
or in another country

The only road I know
is the road to your heart
If you are not beside me, it'll hurt

The only road I know
without you, I am lost...

Cry

cry for people who have been dying from Covid
cry for one who can not change his bad habits
cry for one who can not stop thinking
cry for what is happening
cry for one who has absurd worries
cry for one who can not cry
cry for the world that changes too fast
cry for the past that obsesses our mind
cry for me who dies at last
cry
cry…
(Hanoi 20Aug20)

Ash everywhere

"Hair everywhere" – (Sándor Halmosi)

where there is a man
there is ash
ash from a pipe
ash from a life
ash flies in the sky
ash from a cigarette
ash in an ashtray
ash on a table
ash on a glass
ash in a discussion
ash in a drink
ash in a car
ash in a bar
ash in the air
ash on the hair of a woman
ash in a love affair
ash in space
ash during and after a war
ash in a poetry book
ash from a dead body
ash from misery…

Love seeds

Anna, Anna my dear pearl
You are a beautiful girl
a little girl but a great mind
with your love you give small seeds
the love seeds with little wings that fly anywhere,
to grow hopes and bloom into smiles there...

Drunk afternoon

Bite the sadness
Drink the solitude
I feel the past again

Some pieces of regret
falling down
at the end of the afternoon
Then I smile at the feminine sentimentality

Come here to me
all the ghosts of the past
we all together bottled up
for being drunk

The source

Heaven or earth
paradise or real life
all come from one source
The consciousness of being

Danger

End of the year, I've got a big reward
I want to buy a private airplane
Fly immediately to you in Budapest
You smile and call me Vietnamese James Bond
But without a gun, I can not kill
You smile and tell me that,
my words are dangerous enough for you
that my word can kill, too.
I smile and tell you that,
without love and compassion, it is dangerous, much more…

Changes

habits - cultures
can be good or bad
can be suitable or not
unsuitable habits are not bad
they drive us to change
our old habits to new culture
the interest of life

Peace

knowledge or profit,
not only possess them for yourself,
but share them for all...

That is when my mum is alive
That is when my mum is beside me
That is when I am silent
to hear her familiar voice
to feel her timeless love.

The new truth

The still happiness inside
The active creation outside

27.10.2020
(After the discussion with HJB)

Be alert

We can not see coronavirus

But we can know it, feel it and fear it,

even defeat it

We can not see a mental virus

We rarely know it, rarely feel it and do not fear it,

we also rarely defeat it

But it eats up our energy,

kills us day by day

by our unconsciousness.

Two moons

On my way home after hard work

My legs were heavy but I continued walking

in the dim light

The sun was falling down as usual

to make a normal sunset

I stopped and looked up at the sun

Suddenly I realized it became a red moon

I could look at it easily, even touch it smoothly

And I missed you, my soulmate who lived far away

Might you have looked at the red moon at the same time

rising from your side?

and you called it sunrise?

The red moon brought away my tiredness

brought to you my best wishes

And behind me, another moon, the golden moon was flying in the sky as usual brought to me the whisper from you

I am the golden moon, and you are the red one

We are far away, but together we are in the same way

following each other,

like the two moons,

connecting each other

by the same wish -

just being whole.

Lost in the river of time

I put all my belongings in a backpack

I am going to travel to my garden home

I put on my red shoes

without knowing what I do

Then I am on the bus home

Suddenly I look down and see

the red shoes

Oh the red shoes

How can you be here with my feet

I never imagined it

I walked in you to 5-star hotels

to luxury restaurants

but never ever to a garden

Tomorrow I will put on my red shoes

and walk to my garden

I am lost in the river of time.

Soulmateship

What is higher than love, greater than friendship, more sacred than spouses' possession?

That is soulmates' proximity, accompaniment and association

(16.5.2021)

Pathless

Hanoi was in the distancing time

The streets, lanes were blocked

You called me from the Danube side,

How much we missed each other

We didn't know if we would die before we could meet

But I tried to live,

to build for a better tomorrow which may never arrive

to hold your image inside me

to believe that you still wait for me in Budapest

Together, we would pass the pathless path…

(1/9/2021)

Release myself

Open my eyes and walk in the light

Walk towards "The Unknown"...

Surrender the fate

I accept the spiral of life

(Hanoi 4/4/2022)

Alive word

That word is alive
When I hide it in silence

(Hanoi 26/3/2022)

The beauty of Petofi

Your name is the beauty of Hungarian spirit.

When I read your name Petofi

at the same time, I hear the beauty of my voice.

You lived your dream of Freedom,

for your country,

for the world…

You saw the beauty of everything

from the little cat,

to a golden falling leaf.

You sang the eternal song for all,

and at the same time, you changed the world,

to a real paradise on earth…

The divine emptiness
"Be present" (HJB)

Why meet?

then be forced to part…

Why full moon?

then crescent moon…

Why fill me?

then let me go.

The emptiness

fills me again

The invisible tantra intimacy

reveals itself

at night

and I feel

I am the one inside you.

I can be everyone

at day

Only the emptiness

appears

when it's not night or day

when I am not here or there

I am divided

to be in three worlds,

three states

Awaken to be no one

nowhere

beyond the timeline…

What remains

the sensation of ever-Samadhi

within my stillness.

What remains

just the scent of a fresh mint leaf

that stirs my spirit

Love in moonlight

Love in sunshine

Love is the source of endless energy

Love is the religion of all human beings

Walk into our fate

We share the way

to the infinite

The long walk

is not a complete journey

It reveals our accompanying

The long talk

is not what is wrong or right

It reveals the need

of union

for the two of us

on the journey to our fate.

Flying on golden wings

Connecting our source

when Red River meets Blue Danube

All the birds

rising from forests

All the deaths

rising from darkness

together turn into golden wings in the Light

flying high

above the Parliament Building

above us.

Around and around

Golden wings flying around

welcome a rebirth

of an eternal love

And we see the Light

inside us

The eminent self.

Transcendent union

When our bodies talk
our minds close
our hearts beat wildly

Let our bodies talk freely
Each touch from you to me
awakens a fresh petal

And the whole flower
starts blooming
A wizard in you
finds the Light in me
That I've never seen myself

Our hearts lead
all the kisses to infinite
The bodies connect

The universe unites

Love in Moonlight.

After a pipe

Light up three candles

Burn up a pipeful of herb

The aroma flies around the romantic balcony

Blueberry and lychee

unite on our tongues

After the pipeful of herb burns out,

comes a long kiss.

It's so sweet

Even a hair wants it

and joins in the malt of Sex Whiskey

between our drunken lips

Hair in a kiss again.

After a pipe,

comes a sweet kiss.

It's our sacred ritual -

Love in Moonlight.

Collapse of humanity

Dear little girl,

I know that you are crying

Lots of arrows from the evils

attack you from behind

You are the last Cathars

I am crying here for you, too

But I don't know what to do

I am crying more for myself.

The world collapses in front of me

The more fame I gain

The more loneliness I get

No belief in people around

No way of real living

I have died

before Death comes

in the play of life.

The death

Nothing is important anymore

When we are only silent

Troubled thoughts

Excessive thoughts

bring the Death

erase our feelings

repress our love

We cannot say it out

And you forever can not get over it

Freedom

which you most care about

It will be lost

Even though your heart was crying

And you hide it

Even though I am silent

Compress my anger

You – my illusion

quietly turning your back to me…

Enough!

Everyone needs more

More property

More titles

More victory

More fame

More love

More power

More

and more…

But Mother Nature

can not care for all those

who want more

Mother cares enough

for what she has born…

Cut myself

My mind is a dangerous knife
I cut myself all the time.

Man and Woman

"No woman, no cry"*

"No man, no pain"**

The fight

the union

The kiss

The bite

The smile

The cry

the duality

rolling us

in its game

Just play

until the last breath

by the joy within us.

*By song writer: Vincent Ford

**Song by Felice Tazzini, Marco Guidolotti, and Marco Loddo

Two books

You write a book of the future

The book of thoughts

It brings about sufferings

I write a book of what's happening

The book of the present

It brings about happiness

We are lovers of life

Life is a masterpiece

Live it by our hearts

Create it by our souls

All of us

Master of our minds.

Grape and Rose

Hey Honey

Come and rest on my lap

The long walk at night in Etyek village*

gives us a sweet tiredness

The silver crescent moon

is landing on the grape field

as you are landing in my abnormal life

I need you, my dearest baby

as the Grape needs the Rose

You are the sensitive Rose

in this dangerous world

Who will protect you, my Rose?

* Etyek is a village in Fejer county, Hungary, approximately 30 km from Budapest. The area is surrounded by vineyards and is known for its wine production. (Wikipedia)

Step into the Unknown

I really step into the Unknown

Our love is the Unknown

Every person wants to love someone and wants some others to love her (or him). But what is the real love?

Do we really know how to love ourselves,

how to love people?

We still do not know

We are not true enough to love

We are not brave enough to love

We are not conscious enough to love

One day, I had a very strange journey to Budapest,

And I found a new love, an incredible love

It changed my life, and through me, the world changed.

It is greater than me

It is greater than ordinary life

That is the Unknown.

Summer night at Bartok Bela* street

Summer night,

the full moon

gilds us generously by its silver light

A cool night

A hot night

You hold me from behind,

enter me

from the lips

up and down

little by little

slowly I melt

in a Budapest summer night

and I kiss you all

the summer night is still

for us

the two bodies

have their own way to talk

in rhythm into each other

the Danube river

witnesses the love in silence

the Liberty Bridge

connects the two banks by verses

and the Romance

has just been born.

*Bartok Bela is an old street in Budapest (Hungary)

O man

We cling to what we lost

We pursue what we don't have

O man we don't know what we need

Secret box

Beyond life

Beyond death

An & Andras*

finally find each other

In the Néprajzi Múzeum** of Hungary

The Finnish Divination Box***

Heal their pain from the infinite division

They meet each other in the future

They meet themselves at present

Nodule, claw, smooth stone, berry, twig…****

All the supernatural healing objects

Surround them in a mystic music

They find each other in a unique way

Only the two of them are chosen to be on the way

to the world beyond dualistic mind.

*An & Andras are the 2 main characters in the Novel "The Romance in Budapest" by author Kieu Bich Hau

**Museum of Ethnography in Budapest (Hungary)

*** The secret box which had been used in divining the future, influencing love outcome, warding off evils, conjuring or healing…

**** the mystic objects in the Finnish Divination Box

Danube late afternoon

I leave Hanoi

out of my comfort zone

My soul wakes up

realizes herself in Budapest

You take me out

to downtown.

Having eaten

Dinner in the song of Santa Esmeralda*

and the aroma of arugula rocket leaf.

Lean on a late afternoon

by blue Danube

Sunlight miniates the whole street in golden color

you miniate my soul by your smile

We are side by side

Is it real life now

or only in my dream?

Do we really meet each other

after over three years of separation by Covid?

That song in the street

from the heart of the artist

is for the soulmates

who meet in Budapest

the city of mystic love.

*The song "You're my everything" by Santa Esmeralda

The song of Red River

They used to be soldiers

They are poets, too

They sang in the forest

Their tears fell on sacrificed comrades after battles

Beyond death,

Beyond life

Beyond war

They have lived that poetry trend of Vietnam

Forever Vietnam.

And today by the Red River

We all sing together the eternal love song for them

Ao dai* at Buda castle

When Red River meets Blue Danube

in the deepest current.

A tiny orange wing flies up to Buda castle

A Vietnamese girl in Ao dai

dreaming at the riverside high hill

listening to the whisper of the two rivers.

Hear the secret of soft liberation

of love and compassion

In silence

The tiny orange wing melts in the current

The confluence of the Red River and Blue Danube.

*Ao dai is a Vietnamese traditional dress

Love & Gratitude

(Many thanks to HJB)

You give me love

You give me power

A source for a dreamer

to be a new poet

A new Maija*

being charged by mystic energy,

expressing great gratitude to the Universe

Like a floating iceberg

Marriage is the known above

Love is the unknown below

What we see is floating

What we unsee is infinite,

In love, we are centered

In love, enter the unknown,

our souls

We access our hearts,

access the greatest mystery,

spirit

possibilities,

and Akasha

*Maija – a character in an old Czech film

Boiling sea

The sea is boiling

All species are killed at the same moment

The earth is rolling in the universe as a heat-steamed eye

And you boil me

by your hot tears.

Daily chant

Less quarrel

More zen

Less sitting

More jogging

Less sadness

More laughing Yoga

Eat less

Work more

Hate less

Love more

Less hitting

More caressing

Less breaking news

More poems

Less weapons

More trees

Less consuming

More cleaning

We save the world

SOS

Fix yourself

Before commenting on anyone
Comment on yourself first
Edit what you think,
what you will do.

Correct yourself
It is the right way to correct this world
Open your eyes
Look inside yourself
You will see the universe
And find the balance.

Illusion

In the whole image of you,

a real you is 20%,

another you in my mind is 80%

There is a conflict in me

Beauty and Secret

of loving you.

Hotel President

On the Roof terrace café

of Hotel President

the Tower of St. Stephen's Basilica, Budapest eye, Neo Gothic,

all lightened in the golden sight

Beside each other tonight

we find the stillness

the greatest power

in the universe.

Authentic love is never a mistake

We'd better enjoy our love now

before it melts away

Margarita* leaves salt on my lips

And you drink it from my salty lips

The more you drink it

the more you are thirsty

But you will not cry 30 years later

because we drink these salty drops here right now.

Wisdom

Sit at the lowest place

Do the mission at the highest level

Save your energy for your core work

The historic task is in your hand

Be calm

Don't negate anyone

Each one has his place under the Sun

Don't delete any relationships

You don't know who you will meet at the end of the road

Never strangle any idea

Each one can raise his voice under the Sun

Secret Song of Solitude Soul

On the top of the Museum of Ethnography*

I am not afraid of the great height

when you are beside me

I walk up to the sky

walk into a mist

feel that I am your little Princess

in the land of legend, love and progress

Out of the mist

you enter a photo

when I smile

The moment of beauty is caught

by the smartphone,

stored there forever

like evidence of existence here now

The eternal love for a moment

when my soul sings her secret song…

*Museum of Ethnography in Budapest (Hungary) – Néprajzi Múzeum

The ash in me

Wandering in the Memory
Merging in the Misery
Red River misses Danube
hides the still deep waves

Loneliness tightens the missing
All night staying up waiting
The burning verses written out
Leaving me – the ash down

M.U.M*

On my way to work

I think of you all the time

and miss you much

How are you there, my dearest love?

Do you see how much I love you?

Memory of you nurtures my soul

My soul sings the song of love

while holding eternity in my hand

*M.U.M: miss you much

Never be picky

Use what we have in our hands

Never be picky in anything

Waken the souls in all things around us

Reduce suffering for all species

The simplest is the greatest.

Bat Trang, holding hands

In the flying rain of Spring,

we see the soul of earth.

700 years of a ceramic village,

history tells us more truth than ever.

(Bat Trang ceramic village, Feb/2023)

You are a strong wind

You said, sometimes we need to be fast, sometimes slow,

sometimes noisy,

sometimes quiet

You come to me as a strong wind

And my life suddenly becomes a poem.

You are a strong wind

I am soft water

We move wind into water

in harmony

And so on the waves to the Infinite

Spirit

No energy

No ambition

Not hate

Not love

Just being invisible

flying anywhere

observe what happens

without any touches

without interference

without evaluation

Spirit!

Purification

Grows from the mud of samsara

The lotus blooms into endless love verses

Each petal contains a verse

continues to open

open

open more…

When all other people read those verses

The happiness will be released

The light will shine over

Love grows inside all hearts

from a golden seed,

Leaves emptiness in me

A purification

Just being here right now

HJB

You accidentally fell on me in Hanoi

I didn't know you are HJB*

Until the day I came to Budapest

You looked at me and all my words disappeared

The whole world became a love poem

The wind became soft and sweet

The wave forgot its vibes

A romance by the blue Danube

Although we meet nowhere

In fact, I meet you anywhere I go

Although it may be an impossible meeting

You surely are where I most want to go

and stay forever.

*HJB: Hungarian James Bond

Doless

No need to overturn someone else's rice pot

Nature will filter it

The best fighter not fighting

Senseless

Love

Soul

We all need them

Love is like perfume

When you use it for a long time

You lose its aroma

Your soul is like perfume

When you use it for a long time

It disappears

In fact, your love, soul is still within you

Just you lose your sense

Robots never gets angry

Sometimes people attack me not because of myself,

They have a bomb inside them and it suddenly explodes on me

What can I do with those bombs

What can I do to be invulnerable in front of the devils?

I become a robot, without any emotions

Just smile at all those attacks

And simply say "Thank you" to those people/devils

Robots never gets angry.

Touch you in the distance

I am in Hanoi

You are in Budapest

Between us is a long distance of over ten thousand miles

I miss you every minute

And I can not touch you with my hand

So I touch you gently with my thoughts

Do you feel it, my dearest HJB?

Love you in very long distance

I touch you every time with my thoughts

You are always on my mind

One part in me knows that

I should love you forever in the distance

I should never own you as my lover or my spouse as usual

You are not a thing, but you are everything

We should be free from clinging to each other

But another part of me wants you to be mine

Is that a feminine duality?

Between the two

My mind moves

You are always on my mind

I want to say to you, that I love you and miss you much each day

But I am so afraid that you will be tired of me

And I wonder if you love me so

Then I keep silence, say it in the distance

Hope that you can hear me

even when I don't say anything

Just touch you gently with my thoughts

You are always on my mind.

Living metaphors

1

No condition for freedom

No condition for love

We are human beings

2

More believes

More achieves

3

Do not be a victim

Be a victor

4

Do not be a survivor

Be a creator

5

Where there is a fire, there is a life

And I am water

6

Why worry?

Be a warrior

Pray

The good gives us energy

The evil makes us stronger

Grateful to all!

Call girl
(When heaven bends down to hell)

"Woman on top, woman under bottom" - HJB

From the Cinema hotel

I come to downtown Seoul

Suddenly I find

On a street corner

In the crowded region

Where I can't walk

The girl lying on the road

I care not to step on you

I want to cry

Looking down and pick you up

24 hours a day

Any man can call you

Do they find joy on your body?

Do they reach the pain deep inside you?

Their lust destroys our world

The pain is lying in my heart

And I think of my daughters at home

They are now working in their office

Or smiling with their lovers

Or sleeping happily in the warm bed at home

What about you?

You are lying here on the road

by bare body

by a hotline number for 24-hour sex

anyone can step on you

blurred by tears from my eyes

I bend my knees on the road

And pick you up

Blow the dust from you

Blow the burden and pain from this material world

That' it!

Eyes wide open, eyes closed shut

On a Seoul street corner

The girl lying on the road

A falling leaf in Autumn

The leaf waves to the wind in the sky

The call girl waves to me down on the road

Looking up I see the red leaf waving to the wind

Looking down I see the call girl in a red top waving to my mind, my heart…

I bend down

bend down,

heaven bends down to hell…

A storm of love

Beautiful aromatic body

And passionate kisses

You enter me by your power

I close you in my depth

A storm of love

Two bodies intertwine

Energy releases

Freedom blooms

Can Gio* – the little paradise

Step on sharp broken sea shells cover

It cuts and your toe bleeds

You smile and tell me that it doesn't matter

Gentle waves come to make my hair wet

And I look so sad

A sad girl in the little paradise

Sunlight dyes your skin red

You go into the blue sea

Far away from me

I don't see you amongst millions of white waves

You dive in the rhyme

I write your name on the wet sand

Even water is so curious

Comes up to see my letters on the sand

holds around your name HJB

My heart is full of love

Your soul is full of happiness

You say to me: "Now I know what happiness is"

The eternal moment we've made

The deep memory becomes the source of fulfilment

To get balance in loneliness

A sweet kiss in salty waves

is all what I can give you now

The waves make my hair so wet

The wind blows it dry then

All that happens in Can Gio – our own little paradise

I love you and let you go

Like the sea releases its waves in wind

Wherever you are, it's my little paradise

Time passes by

Time will clear us from this life

The waves come and go

The waves clear your name I wrote on the sand

Only the little paradise stays

stays

stays out of time...

(9Feb.2023)

(*Can Gio is a beach, about 50km from the center of Ho Chi Minh city, Vietnam)

About the Author

Kieu Bich Hau

Member of Vietnam Writers' Association
Born in 1972 in Hung Yen Province, Vietnam
Graduated from Hanoi University for Teachers of Foreign Languages (English Department) in 1993
Certificate of Creative Writing Course by Nguyen Du School for creative writing.
Executive Expert of External Affairs Office of Vietnam Writer's Association (From 2019 until now)
Editor of NEUMA magazine of Romania
Editor of Humanity magazine of Russia
Ambassador of Ukiyoto Publisher of Canada to Vietnam
Managing editor of Vietnam Textile – Garment – Fashion Magazine (From 2011 -2021)
Former Deputy Editor-in-chief of Intellectual Magazine (From 2008 to 2011)

Former Deputy Manager of Editorial Board of New Fashion Magazine (From 1993-2003)
Now living in Hanoi, Vietnam.

6 Awards in Literature:
Literary Award for the Youth in 1992 by Tien Phong Newspaper and Nguyen Du School for creative writing.
Second Award in The short story contest organized by Literature Newspaper in 2007.
Award in the short story contest organized by Military Arts & Literature Magazine in 2009.
Award for the best short story by the Naval Command in 2015
Award for excellent short story by Military Arts & Literature Magazine in 2015.
The ART Danubius Prize in 2022 for her nurturing and deepening Vietnamese-Hungarian literary and cultural relations.

Published 20 books:
- Road of Love (Volume of short stories, 2007)
https://www.vinabook.com/duong-yeu-p25837.html
- Orphaned waves (Volume of short stories, 2010)
https://dongtay.vn/sach/song-mo-coi-6211
- Golden cloud (Volume of short stories, 2011)
https://www.vinabook.com/may-vang-truyen-ngan-p43009.html
- Follow the Lily aroma (Volume of short stories, 2011)
https://tiki.vn/theo-dau-loa-ken-truyen-ngan-p341347.html

- Green Camomile (Novel, 2012)
https://tiki.vn/xuyen-chi-xanh-tieu-thuyet-p344782.html
- The weird dream (Volume of short stories, 2012)
https://tiki.vn/di-mong-p358775.html
- Change the life (Volume of essays, 2014)
https://tonvinhvanhoadoc.net/thay-doi-doi-nguoi-tap-tan-van-cua-kieu-bich-hau/
- Pub of mice (Volume of short stories, 2015)
https://tiki.vn/quan-chuot-p430495.html?src=brand-page&2hi=1
- Roses can not stand in a shrimp paste jar (Volume of short stories, 2017)
https://tiki.vn/hoa-hong-khong-o-cung-mam-tom-p690983.html?src=brand-page&2hi=1
- Smart Wife (Volume of short stories, 2019)
https://tiki.vn/smart-wife-vo-ao-p10501730.html?src=brand-page&2hi=1
- The last song (Selection of poems and short stories, 2019 – English version)
- The Lieutenant General who had worked 9 years in the Dragon House (Life story, 2020)
- The Flying red arrow (Volume of short stories, 2020)
https://dongtay.vn/sach/mui-ten-do-vut-bay-9511
- The Unknown (Volume of bilingual poems: English and Italian by IQdB Edizioni- 2020)
https://www.amazon.it/dp/B08C94RKR2/ref=sr_1_1?__mk_it_IT=%C3%85M%C3%85%C5%BD%C3%95%C3%91&dchild=1&keywords=i+quaderni+del+bardo+edizioni+per+amazon&qid=1593855594&sr=8-1

- The God is within us in the infinite humanity (Volume of short stories, 2021)
- The Swear in Budapest (Novel, 2021)
https://tonvinhvanhoadoc.net/loi-the-budapest-luon-la-chinh-minh-trong-tinh-yeu/
- Where you belong to… (Novel, Youth publishing house, 2022)
- Being Human, being Demon (Novel, Ukiyoto Canada 2022)
- The Fear (translated work, Vietnam Writers' Association' publishing house, 2022)
- 5Sights of Light (Co-published volume of poems, Ukiyoto Canada, 2022)

www.ingramcontent.com/pod-product-compliance
Lightning Source LLC
LaVergne TN
LVHW041624070526
838199LV00052B/3231